Steck-Vaughn
POINT
of
VIEW
Stories

Wake Up,
Rip Van Winkle!

By

Dr. Alvin Granowsky

Illustrated by

Rhonda Childress

STECK-VAUGHN
C O M P A N Y

A Subsidiary of National Education Corporation

"**W**ake up, Father! Wake up, Rip Van Winkle!"
Honestly, when that man is not telling stories, he's
asleep dreaming up new ones. Don't get me wrong.
Father is a kindly man. But he's an idler with no desire
to do anything of practical use. He means no harm, but
he has caused our family no end of embarrassment with
his foolish tales and his idle ways.

Perhaps you have heard his yarn about sleeping in
the mountains for twenty years. Folly and fiddle-faddle!
I'll tell you the real story.

Many years ago, Father was young and energetic.
He spent his days telling stories to his friends while he
helped them with their chores. As long as he had a tale
to tell and a willing listener, Father was a happy soul.

That's why Mother loved him so. Although you may
have heard tales to the contrary, my mother was a
sweet-natured woman. She was absolutely devoted to
Father and never tired of listening to his endless tales.

You may well wonder what happened to that storyteller
Rip Van Winkle and his devoted bride. How did she
come to be known far and wide as the dreaded nag who
made Rip Van Winkle's life miserable? It was all Father's
doing—you'll see soon enough.

Mother adored Father and every tale he told. But Little Rip and I were embarrassed by the foolish things he said. We knew the river couldn't turn into feathers and the sky couldn't rain syrup. We never believed that there was a tree that grew eggs or a mule that could sing.

But folks didn't seem to care how silly Father's stories were. People came from all over the valley to listen to his tales. And Father was happy to entertain any audience. One of his favorite audiences was the group that gathered at Nicholas Vedder's inn each day. Father spent a great deal of time there. In fact, that's where he was when his troubles began.

I had gone to the inn to fetch Father home for dinner.

"How do you think up all those ideas, Rip?" I heard Brom Dutcher ask.

"Why, I pull my best ideas out of the flour barrel," answered Father with a wink, and he immediately began to tell a story about the first idea he ever pulled out of the flour barrel. But a strange thing happened. For the first time in his life, Father couldn't finish the story.

"I just reached way down deep and . . ." Father's face went blank, and he could not make one more word come out of his mouth. Father was more than embarrassed—he was panicked. His listeners were stunned. Rip Van Winkle without a story? Unthinkable!

"Is something wrong?" asked Nicholas Vedder.

"N-n-no," stammered Father. But something was wrong and Father knew it. I knew he couldn't bear the idea of his friends thinking he was out of stories.

"Are you ill?" asked Van Bummel, the schoolmaster.

"Well, I'm not feeling quite myself," Father answered.

"Speak up, man. What's bothering you?" demanded Nicholas Vedder as he puffed frantically on his pipe.

"It's just that I'm upset," Father said. "Yes, I'm a bit upset. You see, Dame Van Winkle has been out of sorts lately. She has been scolding me without mercy."

"Oh, that explains it then," nodded Van Bummel knowingly.

I couldn't believe my ears. My mother scolding Father? Folly and fiddle-faddle! But everyone seemed to believe Father, and it certainly got him out of an embarrassing spot.

As we walked home, Father was quiet and worried. Just as we reached the house, he said, "Judith, fetch my gun. I think I'll take a hunting trip into the mountains."

"What shall I tell Mother?" I asked.

"Hmmm. Tell her I'm going hunting for stories," Father said. Folly and fiddle-faddle! I knew you couldn't hunt stories with a gun.

But that's what Father set off to do. He and our dog, Wolf, stayed up in the mountains for close to a week.

"A fine storyteller needs his inspiration," Mother told us. "Your father will tell the cleverest stories ever when he returns."

When Father came home, he was in a great humor. He was full of stories and stayed at the inn from early morning until dark. Everyone was astonished and delighted with Rip Van Winkle's fantastic new tales.

Mother was delighted, too. She was proud of Father and wanted him to share his stories. While he entertained the villagers, she fed the chickens and milked the cows. She hoed the turnips and painted the fence. When the sun got too hot, she came indoors to scrub the floors and mend the clothes. And all the while, she spoke to Little Rip and me of our good fortune in having a father with such a gift.

But every once in a while, Father's gift left him. He would hesitate, tilt his head, and suddenly the story was lost. Each time this happened, Father was so taken aback that he could think of nothing else to say besides, "It's Dame Van Winkle again. She's been in bad temper lately."

His friends would shake their heads in sympathy, and before long, they were telling stories of their own about Dame Van Winkle's terrible temper.

"Poor Rip Van Winkle," said Van Bummel to his wife. "Dame Van Winkle makes his life unbearable. Just today he was in the middle of an excellent tale about how the finest mattresses are stuffed with fog. Before he could even explain how the fog is collected, he was overcome with thoughts of Dame Van Winkle's nagging. He couldn't say another word. That woman must nag constantly to take all the joy out of a good soul like Rip Van Winkle! And I do believe she even takes a broom to his poor, old dog—just to spite Rip!"

"You don't say! What kind of a shrew would hit a defenseless animal? How does Rip bear life with such a woman?" asked Dame Van Bummel.

How could anyone even dream of Mother harming Wolf? Folly and fiddle-faddle! Mother doted on the animal simply because Father enjoyed the dog's company. Mother made sure Wolf ate as well as we did. And she wouldn't hear of letting the dog sleep outside—she made him a soft bed near the fire. But people began to tell many unflattering stories about Mother. "That shrewish woman has driven the tales right out of Rip's head."

Whenever Father ran out of tales to tell, he and Wolf headed to the woods. Each time, Father stayed there a little longer. But he always returned in fine spirits, eager to share new stories with his admirers at the inn.

Father was changing. He no longer offered to help his friends while he told stories, and he spent a great deal of time sleeping. He claimed dreaming helped him get his stories back, as well as discover new stories to tell. In short, Father no longer did work of any sort. Sweet-natured Mother didn't really seem to mind.

"Why, your father's job is to make people laugh!" she often told Little Rip and me. Folly and fiddle-faddle! Father's job was to tend to his farm and family. Of course, Mother ended up doing all his work for him.

There were a few jobs that Mother found difficult, however. When storm winds blew down the fence, she asked Father to help her mend it.

"I promised Brom Dutcher that today I would tell him how the river came to be crooked. You wouldn't want me to let him down, would you?" asked Father.

"Oh no, of course not, Rip. You go on and tell Brom Dutcher your story," said Mother. "Don't worry about a thing. I'm sure I can manage to fix the fence—Judith and Little Rip will help, too. Maybe you can tell us your story when you get home."

After that, Mother didn't bother asking Father to do things around the farm. He was either asleep dreaming up stories, or down at the inn telling his stories to those who would listen. Little Rip and I did what we could, but we were too little to be much help to Mother. All in all, Mother managed everything quite smoothly—until the day the cows knocked down the fence and trampled the garden.

We were just finishing lunch when we heard a terrible ruckus. We looked out the window in time to see those cows crashing through the corn and into the cabbage patch. We scrambled across the yard to the garden and began stomping and waving sticks and throwing rocks and hollering. When the last cow finally sauntered out of the garden, every stalk of corn was flattened and every cabbage was crushed. Beets and carrots were uprooted, and the entire garden was churned into a muddy mess. There was not a plant left standing. Little Rip and I started to cry.

"What will we eat?" wailed Little Rip. "What will we sell at market? We will have no money!"

Mother didn't say a word. She just sat down in the middle of the ruined garden and cried. At last she said, "I don't want to upset your father, but we must go tell him what has happened."

So we went to the inn. When we got there, we saw a group of people gathered around Father.

"We'll wait until your father has finished his story. This bad news will keep that long," said Mother quietly.

But as we drew near to the crowd, we did not hear Father's voice. Instead we heard other voices saying someone should do something for Rip Van Winkle.

"We can't let this go on," said Nicholas Vedder.

"We must do something," agreed Brom Dutcher.

Father was standing as if stunned. He neither moved nor spoke. Mother was so concerned that she ran up to Father, shook him gently, and cried, "Rip . . . Rip!"

But Father just stood stiff as a tree. His lips were parted as if his next word was frozen between them.

"Rip!" Mother shouted a little louder. "WAKE UP, RIP VAN WINKLE!"

The crowd began to murmur.

"Hear how she raises her voice!"

"There's no call for using that tone!"

Mother never even heard the whispers of those around her. She was pale with worry over Father.

"WAKE UP, RIP VAN WINKLE! WE MUST LEAVE AT ONCE! THERE IS IMPORTANT WORK TO DO AT HOME." This time Mother shouted as loud as she could, but still she could not rouse Father.

People gasped. Some glared at Mother.

"It's heartless the way she speaks to him!"

"The woman's a shrew!"

At last, Father opened his eyes and began to mumble.

"You're through telling stories for today," insisted Mother. "If you don't come with me now, you may not be fit to tell stories for a long while."

Of course, Mother meant Father should go straight to bed so he could rest. But people whispered that Mother had shrieked at Father for telling his stories. From that day forward, all the town was convinced that Mother was the most unbearable kind of shrew.

It soon became clear that Father was not the only one in town with a gift for storytelling. Each time the townspeople repeated what had happened when Mother went to the inn, they made the story worse.

"I saw it all. She threw a terrible fit and nearly knocked Rip down," said one woman.

"I heard it all," said another. "And I was at the other end of town. You could have heard Dame Van Winkle screaming in the next village."

Mother knew nothing of the talk she had caused. She kept Father in bed for days and fixed him special meals. She didn't want to worry Father, so she didn't even tell him that the garden was destroyed.

Day after day, Father waited for his stories to return. He stayed in bed and hoped new tales would pop up in his dreams. He sat up in bed once and called for us.

"I've got a story! Come quickly!" he yelled.

Mother, Little Rip, and I all ran to his bedside. His eyes lit up. He spread his hands as he often did at the beginning of a grand story. But when he opened his mouth, not one sound came out. Father dropped his head in disappointment.

"Don't worry, Rip," soothed Mother. "When you are rested, you will tell the cleverest stories ever." Folly and fiddle-faddle! Father didn't need rest. He needed to get to work and forget about telling silly stories.

But Father was desperate. If he lost his gift, he would never be able to show his face at the inn.

"Dame Van Winkle, I must go on a hunting trip," said Father solemnly. He climbed out of bed, got his gun, and headed up the mountain with Wolf.

"Don't worry, children," said Mother. "Your father always finds wonderful ideas in the woods. In a few days, he'll be back with hundreds of tales to tell."

But many days passed and Father did not return. Finally, Mother decided we must take Father some food and make sure he was safe. We started out one morning and didn't find Father until nearly dark. He was sleeping next to the creek with Wolf by his side.

"Wake up, Rip Van Winkle!" Mother called. "Have you found your stories? Can you come home yet?"

Father blinked and shook his head sadly. "I'm afraid I have lost my stories for good." Folly and fiddle-faddle! How can you lose stories?

But Mother tried to comfort Father. "They'll come back in time. Why don't you come home now?"

"What? Come home without a story to tell? I simply cannot do it. I could never face my friends. I will stay right here until I have something new to tell them."

Mother sighed. She knew his mind was made up, so we went back home.

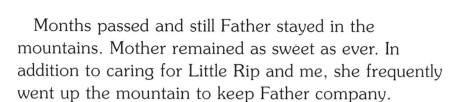

Months passed and still Father stayed in the mountains. Mother remained as sweet as ever. In addition to caring for Little Rip and me, she frequently went up the mountain to keep Father company.

We tried to tell Father all that was going on in the world, but he missed so much! When the trouble with England started, Mother, Little Rip, and I went up to let Father know.

"Wake up, Rip Van Winkle! All your friends are going off to war," said Mother.

"Oh, if only I had a story to tell. I could go along with them and lighten their spirits," Father said.

But he had no story, so he did not come down.

When the war was over, we went up to tell Father about Van Bummel. He had become a great general during the war and was running for Congress.

"Wake up, Rip Van Winkle! Tomorrow is election day," said Mother as she shook Father to wake him.

Father sat up and stretched. "What I wouldn't give for a good tale to tell. Everyone will be gathered on election day, and I could entertain them," he said. Then he added sadly, "But I don't have a thing to tell them."

So election day came and went, and still Rip Van Winkle stayed in the mountains. Through the years, things changed in our little town. Nicholas Vedder died, and a new hotel was put up in place of the old inn. Little Rip grew into a happy-go-lucky young man. Like Father, he preferred hunting and fishing to any kind of work. As for myself, well . . . I found a beau.

We went to tell Father that he simply had to come down for my wedding. We found him stretched out in the grass. He was staring up into the branches of the trees.

"I once knew a story about a tree," he said with a look of deep concentration. "Now, how did it go?"

"Father, I'm going to be married," I said. "Won't you come to my wedding?"

"Everyone will be there," added Mother. "Your friends would love to see you."

Father thought for a minute. "Judith, I wish you the finest wedding day *ever*. But you must understand that a wedding is an important occasion which calls for a *very* special story. I'm afraid I could not bear to disappoint your guests by coming without a fine tale."

No matter how much we insisted, Father would not change his mind. And if missing the wedding wasn't bad enough, Father also missed the birth of my son, Baby Rip. As always, Mother was a great help. She simply adored Baby Rip. How she longed for Father to come home and play with his grandchild!

Mother missed Father terribly. In fact, I do believe that she died of a broken heart. Yes, Mother is gone now. Of course, the townspeople invented their own account of Mother's death—they say she died in a fit of anger. Folly and fiddle-faddle! People just dreamed up that story because they'd heard Father's tales about Mother's temper.

In spite of Father's faults, I still worried about him—especially in bad weather. One evening, a terrible storm hit. The lightning flashed, the thunder rumbled, and the rain poured all through the night. The next morning, I climbed the mountain to make sure Father was all right. When I found him, he was chuckling and slapping his knee as if he had just heard a good joke.

"What a wonderful day this is, Daughter! The most marvelous thing has occurred," he said.

"I haven't seen you this happy in twenty years," I said. "It must take a frightful storm to bring a smile to your face."

"You're not far off. The storm gave me a story. Do you hear? I have a story! And Judith, this is the cleverest story ever. Now run along. I have some thinking to do. I have a feeling there are a hundred stories just waiting to pop back into my head."

I went back to town satisfied that Father was safe, though he was acting even stranger than usual.

Imagine my surprise when I saw Father standing in the middle of town the very next day. He seemed to be causing quite a stir among the townspeople.

"Tell us the rest of the story," begged a little boy.

"Well, after I drank the strange drink, I watched the little men play ninepins. The sound was deafening—as loud as thunder. That's the last thing I remember. I fell into a deep sleep, and I have just awakened this morning. Everything has changed—I am an old man, and nothing in this town looks the same. Twenty years have gone by, yet for me it passed as one night."

When I approached, Father acted as if he had not seen me just the day before.

"Young woman, what is your name?" he asked.

"Folly and fiddle-faddle! You know my name is Judith. What silly game are you playing now?" I asked.

"And your father's name? What would that be?"

"Rip Van Winkle, of course," I replied. "Have you forgotten your own name now?"

"Then this child is my grandchild!" exclaimed Father with delight as he pinched Baby Rip's cheek.

"Tell us another story," called out a woman in the crowd.

"Well now, I just happen to have a few more stories—about twenty years' worth," Father said proudly. "Have you heard about the upside-down house in the forest? That's a good story. And I'll tell it to you sometime. But did you know that there's a rainbow buried in the school yard? That's right, you see . . ."

And Father has been telling those stories down at the new hotel ever since. You'll find him there surrounded by listeners any day of the week. Of course, I don't listen to all that fiddle-faddle. I can't bear to hear his foolishness—he's embarrassed me enough in my life. Still, family is family and he did finally come down from the mountain. So each evening after his storytelling is done, I fetch him from town. I usually find him sound asleep against the steps of the hotel. And I say what we've been saying to him for more than twenty years—"Wake up, Rip Van Winkle! Wake up and come home!"

Steck-Vaughn
POINT
of
VIEW
Stories

Rip Van Winkle

A Classic Tale

Written by
Washington Irving

Retold by
Dr. Alvin Granowsky

Illustrated by
David Griffin

STECK-VAUGHN
C O M P A N Y
A Subsidiary of National Education Corporation

Anyone who has ever traveled up the Hudson River will remember the beautiful Kaatskill Mountains. A part of the Appalachian range, these mountains sit to the west of the river. The mountains stretch out across the countryside while their peaks reach up as if to touch the sky.

At the foot of these mountains stands a little village founded by Dutch colonists. This charming, old village dates back to a time when the country was yet a province of Great Britain, and Peter Stuyvesant was governor of New York.

A simple, good-natured fellow named Rip Van Winkle lived in the village. He was descended from the Van Winkles who had battled bravely at Stuyvesant's side in the quest for territory. Rip, however, had inherited little of his ancestors' nature. Rip was simply a carefree man, always ready with a smile and a story. People throughout the village knew Rip as a kind neighbor and a friendly chap.

Sadly, Rip Van Winkle led the life of a hen-pecked husband. His wife found fault with everything he did. The quarrels between him and his wife raged from early in the morning until late in the evening. From Dame Van Winkle, Rip learned the virtues of patience and suffering.

While his own wife found only fault with Rip, the other wives of the village found much to appreciate in him. The village women always took Rip's part in his family's squabbles and laid all the blame on Dame Van Winkle.

The children of the village adored Rip because he made playthings for them, flew kites with them, and told them long stories about ghosts. Wherever Rip went, children crowded around him. The little ones hung on the man's coat, clamored for his attention, and played countless tricks on Rip. Dogs never barked when this good-hearted man came into their neighborhood.

Rip Van Winkle's tragic flaw in life was his dislike for any type of profitable work. The sad fact was that Rip could have fared well at anything he chose to do. He had patience and endurance. But instead of using those traits to better his situation, Rip was content to sit on a river bank for hours just waiting for a fish to bite. He did not care if he got no more than a nibble. If, by chance, he tired of fishing, Rip would spend the rest of the day wandering through the woods. Perhaps he would come upon a squirrel or some wild pigeons for a meal. It didn't much matter to Rip Van Winkle.

While Rip hated to do any work of his own, he never failed to assist his neighbors with their work. As long as he was doing it for someone else, Rip would take on any task enthusiastically. The man could husk corn and build fences faster than any other man in the village. Whenever they asked, Rip would help the men in the fields or the women in the village. The wives would get Rip to run the errands their husbands wouldn't do for them.

Rip Van Winkle would tend to anyone's business except his own. He found it impossible to manage his own farm. Rip felt that there was no reason for him to work because everything he tried to do went wrong.

Indeed that was how it seemed. The fences on Rip's farm were falling down. His cows were always getting into the cabbages. Weeds grew faster than any corn he planted. This meek man's farm dwindled away under his poor management.

Rip's children fared no better than his farm. They grew as wild and as ragged as the weeds. They didn't seem to belong to anyone. Rip had a son, also named Rip, who clung to his mother's skirts all day. The boy wore his father's old clothes. The pants were so big that little Rip had to hold them up with one hand.

Rip's neglect of his farm and family made his wife angry. One look at her husband loafing about sent her into a tirade. Rip soon learned that there was no use in trying to defend himself. He would simply leave the house.

Not only Rip received the brunt of Dame Van Winkle's anger. Rip's beloved dog Wolf was mistreated, too. Dame Van Winkle blamed the dog for leading his master astray. For that reason, she was always ready to give the poor animal a knock on the head. On a chase through the woods, the dog was fearless, but as soon as Wolf came into the house, his tail drooped.

Times grew more and more difficult for Rip Van Winkle. His wife's sharp tongue grew ever keener from constant use. To escape the misery she caused him, Rip would go to the town inn. On the benches in front of the inn, under a portrait of His Majesty George the Third, Rip would console himself. He passed many a day talking to other idle people such as his friend Brom Dutcher. Usually the group exchanged village gossip. But on occasion, a passing traveler would leave an old newspaper. Then the group would huddle together listening to Derrick Van Bummel, the schoolmaster, read to them. For hours they discussed events that had taken place months before.

Nicholas Vedder, owner of the inn, controlled the opinions of the group. He sat at the door of the inn from morning until night, moving just enough to avoid the sun. The villagers could tell time by Vedder's movements. The man rarely spoke, but he smoked his pipe constantly. If he liked what was being said, he inhaled the smoke slowly. If he did not like what was said, he puffed with great force.

But going to the inn did not ensure that Rip would completely escape his wife. Dame Van Winkle was known to charge into the group and shriek at Nicholas Vedder. She claimed that he encouraged her husband's idleness.

Nicholas Vedder never said a word to the screaming woman. He just sent forth many short, angry puffs of smoke as long as she was present.

His wife's vicious tongue reduced Rip to despair. He would take his gun and retreat into the woods with his faithful dog Wolf. The two seemed to sympathize with one another over their troubles with Dame Van Winkle.

On one such excursion Rip climbed to a green knoll high atop the Kaatskills. Rip spent a fine day enjoying his favorite sport—squirrel hunting. By late afternoon, Rip was tired. He found a beautiful spot to rest. From there he could look down upon the noble Hudson River flowing far below him. As the sun began to set, Rip lay thinking about the beauty of the day.

As Rip prepared to walk down the mountain, he heard a voice calling from the distance, "Rip Van Winkle! Rip Van Winkle!" Rip looked all about but could see no one. As he started to walk on, he heard the voice call once more. Both Rip and his dog stopped. Rip turned around in fear.

Then he saw a strange, little man climbing up the mountain. At first Rip thought it was a neighbor in need of help. But as the little, old man came closer, Rip realized that he was a stranger. The man had a grizzled beard and thick, bushy hair. He wore odd clothes that looked like those of the early Dutch settlers.

The man bore a large, wooden barrel on his shoulders. He motioned for Rip to help him carry it. Although Rip was a bit taken aback by the stranger's appearance, he was always ready to help. Rip hoisted the barrel to his shoulder and started up the mountain. As the two climbed higher and higher, a long, rolling peal of thunder sounded. The thunder surprised Rip because, through the trees, he caught a glimpse of a cloudless, blue sky.

Rip was curious about the small stranger, but continued up the mountain in silence. Finally they came upon a hollow in the woods, like an outdoor theater. Upon entering the clearing, Rip saw an amazing sight. A gathering of odd-looking men were playing ninepins. The little men wore the most unusual clothes, similar in style to those of Rip's companion. They seemed to be amusing themselves, yet their expressions remained serious. Not a sound came from any of them. The only noise to be heard was the balls rolling and crashing against the ninepins. Rip now understood that the game was the cause of the rumbling thunder he had heard.

The odd men stared openly at Rip as if they weren't quite sure what to make of him. Rip's knees began to knock, and his heart quaked. One of the men took the barrel from Rip and poured drinks into large mugs. He motioned for Rip to serve the mugs to the other men. The bearded men took the mugs from Rip's shaking hand. Still not speaking, they gulped down the drink and returned to their game of ninepins.

Little by little, Rip began to relax. He gathered his courage and took a drink from the barrel. As no harm came of it, he took another drink, and then another, and yet another. The strange beverage, whatever it was, tasted better with each gulp. At last, Rip's head slumped against his chest, and he fell into a deep sleep.

Upon waking, Rip discovered himself on the mountain. He rubbed his eyes. Rip saw that it was a bright, sunny morning. Robins were chirping among the bushes as they searched for worms. An eagle soared high above him. Then Rip recalled the strange events that had taken place before he fell asleep. Rip realized that he must have spent the night on the mountain. Where was the strange, little man? Where were the other little men playing ninepins? How would he ever explain this to Dame Van Winkle? Rip sighed deeply just thinking of the rage he faced from his wife.

Rip looked around for his gun. In place of the clean, well-oiled one, he found an old, rusty gun. At once he thought of the bearded, little men playing ninepins. Had they made off with his gun? And where was Wolf? Perhaps he was off chasing a squirrel or a bird. Rip whistled for his faithful dog, but to no avail. Wolf was gone.

Rip planned to find the odd men and demand that his gun and dog be returned to him. As Rip attempted to stand, his right knee creaked and he found that all his joints were stiff. It took a great effort for him to make his way down the mountain trails to the glen below. Rip was sure that the night he had spent in the mountains had not been good for his health.

On his way down the mountain, Rip saw many strange sights. Large rocks he had sat upon were now covered with moss, and huge trees had replaced the saplings he remembered. But he didn't have time to dwell on such matters. He was still upset about his missing gun and dog. But what upset Rip more was the thought of facing Dame Van Winkle. With a heart filled with worry, Rip trudged homeward.

Rip met many people as he approached the village, but didn't recognize any of them. He thought he knew everyone who lived in the countryside, so this surprised Rip. The people were dressed in a style unfamiliar to him. They all stared at him and touched their chins as he passed by. Rip touched his chin, just as they did, and was shocked to find that his beard was over a foot long.

As Rip entered the village, children crowded around him. They pointed at his long, gray beard and laughed. Dogs barked at him as if he were a stranger. Rip knew not one of the children or dogs. The village had changed since he was last there. It had grown larger. Houses now stood in what had been empty fields. Unfamiliar names hung over the doors and strange faces peered out from windows. He thought this was his village, but he must have made a mistake. Rip turned to look around him. There stood the Kaatskill Mountains. There flowed the Hudson River. Both were where they were supposed to be, so this had to be his village. Rip was confused.

Rip even had difficulty finding his own home, but he finally spotted it and went in. He waited in dread for Dame Van Winkle's shrieking, but heard nothing.

Rip saw that his house was in a state of disrepair far worse than he had left it. The roof had caved in, windows were broken, and the door was off its hinges. A half-starved dog was in the front yard. At first, Rip thought it was Wolf, but when he called to him, the dog growled and ran away. "My very own dog has forgotten me!" sighed Rip.

Flustered, Rip left his home to find his old haunt, the village inn. When he came upon it, Rip couldn't believe his eyes. Where the inn had stood, there was now a rickety, wooden building with a sign that said "The Union Hotel." As usual, a crowd of people was gathered at the door. But Rip did not know any of them. Where were all his old friends?

Rip noticed a fellow whose pockets were filled with handbills. The man spouted a fiery speech about the rights of citizens and free elections. The speaker shouted something about Bunker Hill and the Battle of 1776. Rip wondered what it all meant.

The appearance of Rip with his long beard and rusty gun caused people to crowd about him, eyeing him with curiosity. "On which side did you vote?" asked the speaker in an unpleasant tone. Rip stared at him blankly. Then another man stepped up and asked, "Are you Federal or Democrat?"

Rip still did not know what these men were talking about. Silence loomed all around him as everyone stared and waited for his reply. "I am a loyal subject of the king," cried Rip.

That reply caused an uproar. "A tory! The man is a spy! Lock him up!"

The speaker calmed the crowd. Then he asked Rip, "Why are you in our village?"

"I assure you that I mean no harm," Rip said. "I've merely come in search of my friends and neighbors."

The man asked who Rip's friends and neighbors were.

Rip asked, "Where is Nicholas Vedder? This was his inn."

Everyone grew silent. Then an old man replied, "Nicholas Vedder has been dead for over eighteen years."

"And the schoolmaster, Van Bummel?" asked Rip.

"He went off to the war. He was a great general and now is serving in Congress," someone explained.

"What about Brom Dutcher?" Rip asked.

"He didn't return from the war," a man said.

Rip was sad and confused. He asked, "Does no one here know Rip Van Winkle?"

"Of course we know Rip Van Winkle!" exclaimed several bystanders. "That's Rip over there, leaning against that tree."

Rip looked in the direction they were pointing and saw a man who was the image of himself. The fellow looked just the way Rip had when he went up to the mountain.

Rip was now so completely confused that he knew not what to think.

The speaker once again demanded, "Who are you? What do you want here?"

"Heaven only knows!" exclaimed an upset Rip. "I'm no longer me! That's me over there and I've become someone else. I was myself last night. I know that for sure. Then I met some strange, little men playing ninepins, had a drink with them, and fell asleep. When I woke up, everything was different. My gun is different. This village is different. I am different! I no longer know who I am!"

At that, some of the people winked at one another and tapped their fingers against their foreheads. Just then a woman carrying a baby came into the crowd. Frightened by Rip's looks, the baby began to cry. "Hush, little Rip," the woman scolded. "That man won't hurt you!"

The child's name as well as the woman's looks awakened memories for Rip. "What is your name?" he asked the woman.

"Judith Gardenier," the woman replied.

"And your father's name?" he asked urgently.

"His name was Rip Van Winkle," she replied. "Poor man! He went off to the woods over twenty years ago. Nobody knows what happened to him. We only know that his dog Wolf came home without him. I was only a little girl then."

Rip asked one last question in a trembling voice. "Where is your mother?"

"Oh, she died just a short time ago," the woman replied sadly. "She broke a blood vessel in a fit of anger at a New England peddler."

Rip could hold back no longer. "I am your father!" he exclaimed as he hugged the startled woman and her baby.

The crowd was stunned at this bit of news. Then an old woman stood close to Rip and peered into his eyes. "It is Rip Van Winkle!" she exclaimed. "Welcome back, neighbor! Where have you been these twenty years?"

Rip told how his long absence had passed for him as one night. After much talk about how amazing it all was, the gathering broke up, and Rip went home to live with his daughter.

Judith had married a hard-working farmer who was as different from her father as a man could be. In fact, her husband had been one of the little boys who climbed upon Rip's back. Judith and her husband's farm prospered and they lived in a fine, well-kept home.

Rip's son, like his father in every way, was whom Rip had seen leaning against the tree. The young man worked on his sister's farm. Or one could say that he was employed there—he did little work.

Old Rip Van Winkle had reached an age where no one expected him to work. He found some of his old friends to visit, and as always, children flocked to him. Rip spent his days sitting on the bench at the inn much as he had before.

It took some time for Rip to comprehend all the strange events that had happened while he slept away twenty years. The changes in government had little effect on him. He seemed not to care if he was a subject of George the Third or a free citizen led by George Washington. What mattered to Rip was that he was free of Dame Van Winkle.

He loved to tell his amazing story to every stranger that arrived at the hotel. All the old Dutch villagers said it was Henry Hudson, discoverer of that land and river, and his crew whom Rip saw playing ninepins. In fact, every thunderstorm made them think Hudson and his men had returned. It was a common wish of all the hen-pecked husbands of the village that they, too, could watch an odd group play ninepins and enjoy a drink from Rip Van Winkle's barrel.